DIVINE INTERVENTION

FORWARD BY MIKE HUCKABEE

By

Virginia Grace Frost

ISBN: E-Book # 978-1-966556-20-6

Paperback # 978-1-966556-21-3

Hardcover # 978-1-966556-22-0

Printed in United States of America

Library of Congress Reg. # 2025901310

Cover Design by: Authors Hike

Publisher: Authors Hike

Dedication

I dedicate this book to my husband, Russell DeBord, for his invaluable technical support. As a writer, not a techie, I couldn't have completed this book without him. And most importantly, I love him.

Foreword

Divine Intervention, Virginia masterfully captures the essence of hope, resilience, and the transformative power of faith. This is a story of a family's journey through life's trials and tribulations and how their unwavering belief in God not only sustained them but brought them closer to the divine purpose for their lives.

Virginia reminds us all that, even in our darkest moments, God is at work, guiding us toward peace and redemption. Her storytelling is as heartfelt as it is inspiring, and her message is one of hope for those seeking the comfort of faith in uncertain times.

This book is a testament to the fact that trusting in the Almighty can lead us to a life of grace, strength, and renewed purpose. I encourage everyone to read Divine Intervention and let its powerful lessons resonate in their hearts.

Mike Huckabee

Former Governor of Arkansas

Table of Contents

Chapter 1
Understanding Divine Intervention

Divine intervention has always been a powerful theme in my life, shaping not only my experiences but also my understanding of faith, purpose, and the mysteries of existence. For many people, divine intervention brings to mind images of miraculous events or sudden life changes. To me, it feels more personal. I define divine intervention as God actively influencing and guiding my life—a consistent presence of divine support in my daily experiences. Looking back on my journey, I realize that these moments of divine guidance are not just random luck; they come together like a beautiful picture made of faith, hope, and meaningful experiences with the divine.

My journey into understanding divine intervention started with some early experiences that seemed to stand out from the rest. One of the most profound moments happened one restless night when I woke up suddenly, feeling an urgent presence around me. I distinctly heard a voice in my mind saying, "Marry me, marry me; the boys really need you!" This unexpected message struck me deeply. I began to reflect on my life and purpose. Even though I was happily married to a wonderful man and had raised my sons to be independent, I couldn't shake the feeling that there was something more I needed to do. It dawned on me that perhaps God was calling me to help others, to act as a conduit for bringing people closer to Him.

Several significant events in my life have illustrated the role of divine intervention. The first was meeting my husband, which turned out to be a pivotal moment for me. I never imagined marrying a man younger than myself, yet here I was, with someone who was thirty years my junior. This relationship changed my life profoundly, challenging societal expectations and my own beliefs about love and companionship. I realized that divine intervention often comes in unexpected forms, guiding us toward experiences that enrich our lives in ways we could never have anticipated.

Another important moment was when I decided to write my first book. At first, I had no idea how to even begin. The thought of sharing my story felt overwhelming. But as I took the first steps, opportunities started to present themselves. I met supportive people who encouraged me and offered their insights. It was almost as if divine forces were aligning, guiding me toward something I had never thought possible. Finally, I successfully published my first book, which felt like a tremendous gift from God. This experience reinforced my belief that divine intervention often comes with a sense of purpose, helping us navigate through life's uncertainties.

One particularly eye-opening experience occurred on July 13, 2024, when former President Donald J. Trump narrowly escaped an assassination attempt. Watching this unfold in real-time filled me with a sense of divine presence at work. I truly believed that a guiding hand was protecting him, reinforcing my faith that God intervenes during critical moments in our lives. Events like these remind me of the importance of recognizing the divine, especially in chaotic times.

As I explore the concept of divine intervention further, I realize that it is essential to understand the theological perspectives that shape our views. Different religions interpret divine intervention in various ways. In Christianity, for example, it is often viewed as God's love and grace actively present in our lives. Miracles—like healing the sick or guiding someone through difficult times—are seen as manifestations of God's power. Growing up in a Christian household with a Jesuit father deeply influenced my views on faith and divine guidance.

In Islam, divine intervention is seen as Allah's mercy, where God helps individuals through signs, dreams, and answered prayers. The concept of "Tawakkul," or relying on God, emphasizes the belief that placing trust in Allah will help individuals overcome life's challenges. Hinduism presents another perspective, viewing divine intervention as closely linked to karma—the idea that our past actions shape our present circumstances. In this faith, divine intervention serves as a guiding force, helping us navigate the complexities of life while striving for spiritual growth.

To illustrate the power of divine intervention, I think of historical figures who have attributed their successes to divine guidance. Mother Teresa comes to mind. Known for her tireless work among the poor and destitute in India, she often spoke about experiencing divine intervention throughout her life. She believed God directed her to serve those in need, and her unwavering faith inspired many to follow her example.

Another inspiring figure is Martin Luther King Jr., a leader in the American civil rights movement whose life was deeply rooted in faith. Throughout his journey, he often spoke about how his belief in God guided his actions and decisions, providing him with the strength to confront injustice and advocate for equality. King faced tremendous challenges, including threats to his life and imprisonment, but he maintained a profound sense of purpose and hope. He believed that divine intervention was at work in his life, helping him to rally people around a shared vision of justice and love.

In his famous "I Have a Dream" speech, King painted a powerful picture of what a just society could look like. He invoked a vision of divine justice, calling for unity among all people, regardless of race or background. His words echoed the biblical principles of love, compassion, and equality, reminding us that we are all created in the image of God. By emphasizing love and understanding, King illustrated how divine intervention can inspire us to rise above hatred and division.

Both Mother Teresa and Martin Luther King Jr. exemplify how divine intervention can lead individuals to achieve remarkable things, reminding us that we are not alone in our struggles. Their lives encourage us to trust in God's plan, especially when we face obstacles. Just as they found strength in their faith, I, too, have experienced moments where I felt guided and supported by a higher power. Their examples reinforce the theme of this book: that divine intervention is present in our lives, guiding us toward our true purpose. By sharing my own experiences alongside theirs, I hope to inspire others to recognize the divine presence in their own journeys and to understand that, no matter how difficult the path may seem, we are never alone.

As I reflect on my understanding of divine intervention, I realize that it has evolved over time. Initially, I viewed these moments as isolated incidents—brief flashes of divine presence that provided clarity when I needed it most. However, with each significant event, whether it was meeting my husband or witnessing pivotal moments in history, I began to see a pattern. The consistency of these experiences has solidified my belief in divine guidance and has inspired me to deepen my understanding of faith.

Growing up, my father's journey from an aspiring priest to a devoted family man significantly shaped my beliefs. His passing, alongside my mother's, impacted my life profoundly. I believe my father's death was closely tied to his deep emotional bond with my mother. This experience led me to reflect on love, loss, and divine presence.

I often see the moments I have shared as miracles that illustrate divine intervention at work. Writing my first book, meeting my husband, and witnessing important events serve as reminders of the divine presence surrounding me. While I have not personally experienced doubt about divine intervention, I understand that skepticism exists, particularly among younger generations. One of my sons questions the existence of souls and often shares his skepticism with me. His doubts challenge me to deepen my understanding and articulate the importance of faith. These conversations prompt me to explore belief and the mysteries of existence, showing that faith is not a straightforward journey; it is filled with twists and turns.

In my daily life, I do not actively seek divine intervention, but I remain aware of its presence. This awareness encourages me to approach each day with gratitude and an open heart. Though I may not engage with the world as actively as I once did, I find comfort in prayer and meditation. These practices allow me to connect with the divine, inviting guidance into my life. I have made a conscious effort to include Donald J. Trump in my nightly prayers, feeling this is a call for divine guidance. I recognize the complexity of his role in the world, yet I believe that everyone deserves prayers for wisdom and understanding as they navigate their paths.

The experiences I've shared have helped me face significant challenges, providing direction and comfort during difficult times. The knowledge that I am not alone in my struggles—that divine presence surrounds me—has given me strength when faced with life's uncertainties. Each perceived moment of divine intervention serves as a beacon of hope, reminding me to stay strong in my faith and trust the journey ahead.

Throughout my life, I have faced decisions that required careful thought and faith. One significant decision was to include Donald Trump in my nightly prayers. This choice came from a deep belief that he, too, deserves divine guidance, regardless of differing opinions about his actions or policies. It serves as a reminder that faith transcends political beliefs, and we are called to pray for one another, fostering a spirit of unity and love.

I perceive signs of divine intervention through my life experiences, recognizing that I have lived a life that aims for goodness. The moments of clarity and unexpected blessings all point to a greater purpose at play. Divine intervention may not always appear dramatically; sometimes, it shows up in the quiet moments of reflection, urging us to appreciate our journey and the lessons learned along the way.

As I continue to navigate my understanding of divine intervention, I often think about how this awareness contributes to my personal growth. While I may not know its direct impact, I recognize that the more I engage with these experiences, the deeper my faith becomes. The lessons I learn from divine guidance shape my understanding of love, purpose, and the interconnectedness of all beings.

My faith encourages me to view divine intervention through the lens of love for everyone. This love opens my heart and mind, allowing me to experience the presence of the divine in the world around me. It inspires me to approach life with compassion and empathy, recognizing that we are all on our journeys, seeking guidance and understanding. In a world filled with uncertainty and division, my faith serves as a guiding light, reminding me of the importance of love and connection.

As I share these stories about divine intervention, I want to spread the message of God's presence in our lives, using my own real experiences to show His love and guidance. Each story, each moment of clarity, and every surprise blessing has helped shape my faith and understanding, reminding me that we are never truly alone on our journeys. By sharing these personal moments, I hope to inspire others to notice the divine hand in their own lives and to feel a deeper connection to God. My wish is that through these words, readers will find hope, encouragement, and the strength to embrace the divine in their own experiences.

Chapter 2
The Role of Faith in Daily Life

Faith has always been more than just a belief system for me; it has served as a guiding principle that influences my decisions, shapes my actions, and gives meaning to my daily experiences. In this chapter, I will explore how faith manifests in my everyday life, detailing transformative experiences that have deepened my spiritual understanding. I will also discuss the challenges I and many others face in maintaining our faith and share practical exercises that have helped me strengthen my connection with the divine.

Faith has an incredible ability to shape our perspectives, guide our choices, and influence our interactions with others. In my life, I have often turned to faith during pivotal moments, allowing it to illuminate my path forward. Whether making personal decisions, navigating relationships, or facing unforeseen challenges, my faith has acted as a compass, guiding me through complexities and uncertainties.

I vividly recall a time when I was faced with a significant career choice that could alter the course of my life. After years of working in a field that, while stable, felt increasingly unfulfilling, I began to contemplate a drastic change. I felt a call to write—a passion that had always simmered beneath the surface but had never fully emerged. However, the fear of uncertainty loomed large. What if I failed? What if my words didn't resonate with others? It was during this time of doubt that I turned to prayer, seeking guidance from God.

In those quiet moments of reflection, I felt a profound sense of reassurance wash over me. I realized that my decision was not merely about my personal aspirations but was intrinsically linked to a higher purpose. My faith prompted me to consider not just what I wanted but what I believed I was being called to do. The clarity that emerged from prayer encouraged me to take a leap of faith, embracing the unknown with trust in God's plan. Ultimately, I chose to pursue writing seriously, and this decision opened doors I never imagined possible.

Another example of faith guiding my decisions came during a difficult family situation. My son was struggling with a significant life challenge that left him feeling lost and overwhelmed. As a parent, it was heartbreaking to witness his struggles. I felt an intense desire to protect and shield him from pain, yet I knew I could not solve his problems for him. In this moment of helplessness, I turned to faith for guidance. I began to pray for him, asking for divine wisdom to navigate this difficult time.

Over time, I noticed a change—not just in him but in myself. My faith shifted my perspective from feeling overwhelmed and anxious to fostering an attitude of patience and understanding. I learned to listen more and provide support without imposing my solutions. This shift in approach reinforced my belief in the power of faith as a guiding principle. It reminded me that sometimes, the most significant impact we can have on others is through our unwavering support and belief in their capacity to overcome challenges.

Throughout my life, I have encountered numerous transformative experiences that have reshaped my understanding of faith and its role in my daily existence. These moments serve as profound reminders of how faith can lead to personal growth, resilience, and a deeper connection with the divine.

One particularly transformative experience occurred during a challenging period in my life when I was grappling with the loss of my father. His passing left a void that was difficult to navigate, and I found myself questioning the purpose of life and the existence of divine support. In the days following his death, I felt an overwhelming sense of grief and despair, struggling to find meaning in the pain.

It was during one of my most challenging days that I decided to visit a local church. I sat in the quiet sanctuary, surrounded by flickering candles and soft light, and allowed myself to feel the weight of my emotions. As I prayed, I found solace in the stillness, feeling a sense of connection to something greater than myself. In that moment, I experienced a profound revelation: my father's love and teachings would always remain with me, guiding me even in his absence. This understanding transformed my grief into a celebration of his life and the legacy he left behind.

Another significant moment of transformation occurred when I began volunteering at a local shelter. Initially, I approached this experience with a sense of obligation, wanting to give back to my community but unsure of how to engage meaningfully. However, as I interacted with the individuals seeking support, I was struck by the resilience and strength they exhibited. Each story I heard was a testament to the human spirit's ability to endure and overcome adversity.

Through these encounters, I began to see faith manifest in unexpected ways. I witnessed the power of hope as individuals faced their challenges with unwavering determination, often expressing gratitude despite their circumstances. These experiences transformed my understanding of service; I realized that it was not merely about giving but about connecting with others, sharing love, and extending compassion. Volunteering became a source of inspiration, and my faith deepened as I recognized that, in serving others, I was embodying the love and guidance I sought from God.

While faith has played a crucial role in guiding my life, I recognize that maintaining faith is not without its challenges. Many individuals encounter struggles that can shake their beliefs and make it difficult to trust in a higher power. These challenges are often compounded by life's unpredictability, societal pressures, and personal doubts.

One common struggle many face is the experience of unanswered prayers. In moments of deep longing or distress, we often turn to faith, praying for guidance or relief. However, when our prayers seem to go unanswered, it can lead to feelings of disillusionment or despair. I have encountered this challenge myself during times of crisis when I felt abandoned by God.

One such experience arose when a close friend faced a serious health crisis. As I prayed fervently for her recovery, I held onto hope and faith. However, as time passed and her situation worsened, I found myself grappling with feelings of helplessness and frustration. How could a loving God allow such suffering? In this moment of doubt, I realized the importance of acknowledging my feelings and seeking support from my faith community. Through conversations with fellow believers, I learned that doubts and questions are part of the spiritual journey and that wrestling with these feelings can lead to a deeper understanding of faith.

Another challenge I have faced is the influence of societal expectations. We live in a world filled with differing beliefs and perspectives, where faith is often met with skepticism. This can create an internal conflict, especially for those who feel strongly about their beliefs. I have experienced moments when my faith has been challenged by the opinions of others, particularly among younger generations who question traditional values and religious practices.

In conversations with my son, I often encounter his skepticism regarding faith and spirituality. While his questions can be challenging, they also serve as opportunities for meaningful dialogue. Engaging in these discussions encourages me to explore the foundations of my beliefs and articulate the importance of faith. These moments remind me that faith is not static; it evolves as we confront doubts and seek understanding.

Recognizing the challenges to faith is crucial, but equally important is finding ways to strengthen and nurture our beliefs in daily life. Through my journey, I have discovered several practical exercises that have proven beneficial in deepening my faith and fostering a sense of connection to the divine.

One of the most powerful tools for strengthening faith is the practice of prayer. Prayer is not merely a ritual but a genuine conversation with God, allowing us to express our thoughts, fears, and desires. I have found that setting aside time each day for prayer creates a sacred space for reflection and connection.

When I pray, I often begin by expressing gratitude for the blessings in my life, no matter how small. This practice of gratitude shifts my perspective, reminding me of the abundance surrounding me. Following this, I pour out my heart, sharing my concerns and seeking guidance. I have learned that prayer is not always about receiving answers but about cultivating a relationship with the divine.

Additionally, incorporating prayer into my daily routine has allowed me to maintain a sense of mindfulness throughout the day. I often take moments during my day to pause and offer silent prayers—whether it's during my morning commute or while preparing meals. These small moments of connection serve as reminders of God's presence in the mundane aspects of life.

Meditation has also become an essential practice in my spiritual journey. This discipline encourages mindfulness and stillness, allowing me to quiet the noise of everyday life and connect with my inner self. I often begin my meditation practice by finding a comfortable space, closing my eyes, and focusing on my breath.

Through meditation, I have discovered a deeper understanding of faith that transcends words. It allows me to listen and be receptive to divine guidance, creating a sense of peace and clarity. During these moments of stillness, I often find myself reflecting on scripture or spiritual teachings, letting their wisdom wash over me. This practice has deepened my awareness of God's presence and provided comfort during challenging times.

Engaging with a community of like-minded individuals is essential for nurturing and strengthening one's faith. Being part of a supportive network provides encouragement, accountability, and shared experiences that enrich our spiritual journeys. Regularly attending worship services fosters a sense of belonging and connection. I find that gathering with others to worship, sing, and pray reinforces my faith and uplifts my spirit.

Participating in small groups or Bible studies allows for intimate discussions and exploration of faith. Engaging with others in this way enables the sharing of personal testimonies, insights, and questions, leading to a deeper understanding and encouragement as we navigate our spiritual journeys together. Volunteering in the community is another powerful expression of faith in action. I have found that serving others not only allows me to give back but also connects me with individuals who share similar values. Whether at a local shelter or a community event, these experiences serve as reminders of the importance of love and compassion in our faith journey.

I also value the opportunity to participate in faith-based events such as retreats, workshops, or conferences, which provide avenues for spiritual growth and renewal. These gatherings often feature speakers, discussions, and activities that inspire and challenge attendees to deepen their faith. Furthermore, creating or joining a prayer group can foster a sense of accountability and shared purpose. These gatherings often focus on collective prayer and support for one another, reinforcing the idea that we are not alone in our struggles and triumphs.

In conclusion, the practical exercises of prayer, meditation, and community engagement serve as essential tools for strengthening one's faith in daily life. These practices not only foster a deeper connection with the divine but also provide support and encouragement as we navigate life's challenges. By intentionally incorporating these exercises into our routines, we can cultivate a more profound sense of faith and purpose, empowering us to face each day with hope and resilience. As I continue to explore and engage with these practices, I am reminded that faith is a journey—a dynamic process that evolves as we grow and learn, ultimately guiding us toward a more profound connection with ourselves and the divine.

Chapter 3
Overcoming Doubt and Fear

There was a time in my life when I felt completely abandoned by God. As a Catholic woman married to a man who struggled to find consistent work, I was drowning in the responsibilities of raising five children. Financial worries consumed my thoughts. We could hardly make ends meet, and I often found myself sitting alone at the kitchen table late at night, staring at bills and feeling utterly lost. I questioned whether God truly had a plan for us. Why was He allowing this to happen? It was in these dark moments that doubt crept in, whispering lies in my ear and tempting me to turn away from my faith.

The turning point came during one fateful confession. I remember sitting in the small, dimly lit confessional, feeling vulnerable and exposed. I confessed to the priest that my husband and I had stopped using birth control, which went against the Catholic teachings I had been raised with. Instead of compassion, the priest told me to leave the confessional and say three Our Fathers and two Hail Marys. As I walked out of the church that day, I felt abandoned by God. *If God is good,* I thought, *then why would He expect me to sacrifice my health and well-being for a life that feels impossible?* Exhausted and skeletal from the weight of my responsibilities, I couldn't reconcile the teachings of the Church with the reality of my life.

At that moment, I decided to step away from the Catholic Church altogether. It felt like a rejection of everything I had been taught, but I was desperate to find solace. I wandered through a spiritual desert for several years, searching for something—anything—that could restore my faith. Eventually, I discovered the 7-Day Adventist Church, and it was there that I began to feel the flicker of hope reigniting within me. The community was warm and welcoming, and the messages of love and acceptance resonated deeply in my heart. I began to understand that faith could coexist with doubt and that questioning was a part of the spiritual journey.

As I reflect on those years, I realize that doubt and fear often emerge when we feel the most vulnerable. The moments of uncertainty are part of being human, and I had to remind myself that God understands our struggles. He does not abandon us in our darkest hours; rather, He invites us to seek Him out. This realization took time and reflection, but it was profoundly healing.

My journey didn't just involve spiritual struggles. I faced significant physical challenges, particularly as I aged. I have always been an active woman, full of energy and life. However, a severe fall in my home left me grappling with mobility issues. My husband, who is thirty years my junior, stepped into the role of caregiver. At first, I was uncomfortable with the age difference, feeling self-conscious and worried about how it would affect our marriage. I wanted to be strong, to support him, but instead, I felt weak and helpless. I searched for companionship with men closer to my age, but it was always the younger ones who noticed me. I realized that the love we share was part of a divine plan, one that I had not fully grasped until then.

When we first married on August 25, 2006, our lives were filled with adventure. We hiked through forests, danced under the stars, and created memories that warmed my heart. But my accident changed everything. I remember the day I fell vividly; the sharp pain that shot through my body and the fear that washed over me. I was scared, not just for myself but for my family. I worried about my ability to care for them and how my husband would manage. Would he grow resentful of my limitations? Would he feel trapped in a life he hadn't signed up for?

In those early days of recovery, my husband was my rock. He helped me navigate the challenges of physical therapy and patiently supported me as I struggled to regain my strength. He would sit by my side, holding my hand during difficult sessions, reminding me that I was not alone. His love and dedication served as a reflection of God's love—unconditional and steadfast. Slowly, I began to understand that my limitations did not define me; rather, they were part of my journey.

My father's influence also played a crucial role in my spiritual life. He was a man of deep faith, someone who knelt beside his bed every night to pray until he was too weak to do so. His devotion left an indelible mark on my heart. I often think back to my childhood when he would take my small hand in his and walk me to church. Those moments instilled a sense of reverence and connection to something greater than ourselves. Even in my darkest hours, I could hear his voice encouraging me to lean on my faith. I realized that prayer had been my lifeline, connecting me to God even when I felt disconnected from the Church.

Now, as I lie in bed each night, I whisper my prayers into the darkness. This nightly ritual has become sacred for me. I feel closer to God when I'm enveloped in the quiet of the night, sharing my worries and hopes. My husband sleeps beside me, and although he cannot always understand my whispered words, he supports me. In those moments of vulnerability, I feel God's presence surrounding me, comforting me as I navigate my fears.

While I once doubted God's goodness, I now recognize that He was with me all along. When my husband lovingly prepares footbaths to soothe my aching feet, I see the hand of God working through him. These small acts of kindness remind me that divine love often comes to us through the people we cherish. It's easy to overlook these moments, but when I take a step back, I can see the beautiful tapestry of my life being woven together. Each challenge has strengthened my faith and shown me the resilience of the human spirit.

Navigating through adversity has deepened my understanding of what it means to have faith. I've learned that faith is not merely a shield against life's struggles; it is a source of strength that allows us to rise above our circumstances. In my lowest moments, when I felt like giving up, I discovered an inner resolve that I didn't know existed. I found hope in the most unlikely places, whether it was through a kind word from a stranger or the laughter of my children. These moments reminded me that life, even amidst suffering, is filled with grace.

I often think of the statistics surrounding faith and resilience. Studies have shown that individuals with strong faith tend to cope better with life's challenges. Research conducted by the American Psychological Association indicates that spirituality and religious practices can enhance mental health, reducing feelings of anxiety and depression. This has been true for me as well; through prayer and community, I have found healing and support. It's a testament to the idea that we are not meant to walk this path alone.

As I continue my journey, I have come to appreciate the importance of connection—both with God and with others. Engaging with my community at the 7-Day Adventist Church has been a source of strength. Sharing my experiences with others who have faced their own battles has created a bond that transcends words. We gather to share our struggles and victories, reminding each other that we are never truly alone. This fellowship nurtures our spirits and allows us to draw strength from one another.

I have also embraced the practice of mindfulness and meditation. Taking a moment each day to breathe deeply and reflect has become essential for me. In those quiet moments, I can center myself and connect with God on a deeper level. I often find that my fears and doubts dissipate when I focus on the present moment, reminding myself that God is here with me every step of the way.

Moreover, I have found solace in serving others. Volunteering within my community has shown me the incredible resilience of the human spirit. I have met people who have faced unimaginable hardships yet continue to radiate hope and strength. Their stories inspire me to appreciate the blessings in my own life and to cultivate gratitude daily. In serving others, I have discovered a sense of purpose that has further enriched my spiritual journey.

As I look back on my life, I am grateful for the struggles that have shaped me. Each challenge has been an opportunity for growth, a chance to deepen my relationship with God and with those around me. I understand now that faith is not about having all the answers; it's about embracing the questions and seeking connection in the face of uncertainty.

The road may still have its ups and downs, but I have learned to walk it with faith. Each night, as I whisper my prayers, I feel a profound sense of peace wash over me. I have come to know that God is not distant; He is here, guiding me through the storm. I continue to seek His presence in my life, leaning on my husband, my community, and the love that surrounds me. I know now that I can face whatever comes my way, for I am not alone.

In sharing my journey, I hope to inspire others who may be wrestling with doubt and fear. Life can be overwhelming, but in those moments, we must remember that we are not alone. God is with us, inviting us to seek Him out, to lean into our faith, and to embrace the love that surrounds us. Our stories, filled with struggles and triumphs, are all part of a beautiful tapestry woven by the hands of a loving Creator. As I continue to navigate this journey, I hold onto the promise that faith can lead us through even the darkest nights into the light of hope and healing.

Chapter 4
Recognizing Signs of Divine Presence

There are times in life when we feel a nudge—a gentle stirring in our hearts that we can't quite explain. Sometimes, we experience moments so perfectly timed they feel beyond coincidence, leading us to wonder if a force larger than ourselves might be guiding us. Recognizing signs of divine presence can be an awakening experience, one that transforms our understanding of faith and deepens our connection with the divine. I've come to realize that these signs can take many forms, from profound life events to subtle, quiet whispers gently urging us to pay attention.

Throughout my life, there have been moments where I felt something beyond myself—a presence guiding me, calling me, or providing comfort when I needed it most. Yet, just as often, I found myself questioning: Was that truly a sign from God, or merely coincidence? How could I discern the difference? Over time, I've learned that recognizing divine signs isn't always straightforward. It requires patience, openness, and a willingness to trust in a greater plan. In this chapter, I want to share what I've learned about the different types of signs, how to distinguish them, and how personal experiences, journaling, and reflection can help us tune into the messages God may be sending us.

Divine signs come in various forms. Some are clear and undeniable, leaving us with a sense of awe and wonder. Others are subtle, nearly imperceptible, requiring quiet attentiveness to notice. I've found that divine signs often appear during pivotal moments—when we're grappling with doubt, facing a difficult decision, or feeling particularly vulnerable. But they can also come as quiet reassurances, present in the smallest of details.

Some divine signs manifest through major life events that shake us to our core. These might be sudden changes in our path, unexpected losses, or unforeseen opportunities. When my father passed away, I was overcome with grief and a sense of abandonment. But shortly after his passing, I had a vivid dream where he stood beside me, radiating peace and reassurance. It was as though he were saying, "I am with you, and so is God." I woke up feeling comforted in a way that words alone could never convey, and I understood this as a sign, a reminder that I was not alone, even in loss.

For others, major events might include miraculous recoveries, like someone surviving an accident against all odds or even meeting someone who changes the course of their life. I have a close friend who shared a story with me about narrowly avoiding a terrible car accident. She had been running late, frustrated, and caught in traffic. But that delay ended up saving her from being at the exact spot where a major collision occurred minutes later. To her, it wasn't just luck—it was divine intervention. She took it as a reminder to slow down, to be present, and to trust that sometimes, delays and setbacks can serve a greater purpose.

Divine signs don't always come with grandeur; many are like whispers, barely noticeable at first. I believe that God speaks to us through these gentle nudges, encouraging us, guiding us, or even cautioning us. One morning, as I was preparing to leave the house, I felt a persistent urge to call a friend I hadn't spoken to in years. We'd grown apart over time, and I hesitated, not wanting to disrupt her day with an unexpected call. But the feeling didn't fade, so I decided to reach out. When she answered, her voice broke. She told me she had been struggling, feeling isolated and alone, and my call had come at the exact moment she needed someone to talk to. This was no mere coincidence; it was a subtle nudge, a sign that God had been listening to her silent prayers.

These small, quiet signs often appear in ordinary moments, but they can carry profound meaning. The feeling of peace after a difficult prayer, the way a certain verse stands out when reading scripture, or even a song that plays on the radio just when we need it most—all these can be signs of divine presence if we are open to recognizing them.

Coincidences are perhaps the trickiest signs to interpret. How do we know if they are random or if they're a message meant for us? I remember a time when I was struggling to make a decision about my career. I prayed, asking God for guidance, but I didn't expect an immediate answer. The next day, I was at the library, absentmindedly browsing the shelves, when a book fell at my feet. The title? *Finding Purpose in Your Work*. The book contained exactly the wisdom I needed at that moment, with passages that resonated deeply. I could have brushed it off as a strange coincidence, but something inside me felt that this was a gentle nudge from above, reminding me to trust in a purpose beyond what I could see.

Recognizing divine signs is a unique experience, and for each of us, it can look different. There are a few stories that I remember from individuals who've shared their moments of divine connection with me, each a witness to the uncountable ways God reveals His presence.

One that I remember at the top of my mind was Angela, a mother of two who found herself overwhelmed by life's demands. She was caring for her ailing mother, working long hours, and struggling to balance it all. One evening, she prayed, feeling utterly defeated. "God," she whispered, "please show me I'm not alone." The next day, while running errands, she met a woman at the grocery store who struck up a conversation with her. This stranger turned out to be a counselor who specialized in helping caregivers find support networks. Angela felt that this was not an accident but an answer to her prayer—a reminder that God listens and places people in our lives just when we need them.

Then there was this guy named Tom, a retired veteran, who shared with me how he had always dreamed of reconciling with his estranged son, but pride and old wounds kept him from reaching out. One day, as he sat in a quiet park, a young father with a small child sat beside him. The man struck up a conversation, and as they talked, Tom felt an overwhelming sense of familiarity and compassion. Before leaving, the young man said, "If there's someone you need to reach out to, don't wait too long." Tom took it as a sign and, after years of silence, called his son. To his surprise, his son welcomed the contact. Their relationship began to heal, and Tom credits that chance meeting as a divine sign—a reminder from God to let go of pride and seek connection.

The stories of Angela and Tom teach us that divine signs often appear in our moments of need, reminding us that we are never alone. Unexpected encounters can serve as powerful messages from God, encouraging us to take action and seek healing or reconciliation in our lives. These narratives highlight the importance of being open to the guidance of others and trusting in divine timing, showing that God often communicates through people and situations to lead us toward support and connection. Ultimately, they remind us to stay vigilant for signs of divine presence in our everyday experiences.

One of the greatest challenges in recognizing divine signs is discerning whether something is genuinely from God or simply a coincidence. It's easy to doubt ourselves, to brush off these experiences, or second-guess the meaning behind them. Discernment is a practice that requires patience, openness, and a willingness to listen.

To discern between coincidence and divine intervention, I've found that tuning into my inner feelings is essential. Divine signs often carry a sense of peace or clarity. If I feel an overwhelming sense of calm or an inner conviction, I'm more likely to trust that this is God's guidance. On the other hand, if a moment leaves me confused or uncertain, I remind myself that it's okay to seek further clarity through prayer and reflection.

Another important aspect of discernment is patience. Sometimes, the meaning behind a sign isn't immediately clear. In these moments, I try to stay open, trusting that God will reveal His intentions in time. I also remind myself that God's guidance often aligns with His values of love, compassion, and kindness. If a sign encourages these qualities, I am more inclined to believe it is from Him.

One of the most valuable practices in recognizing and understanding divine signs has been keeping a journal. By writing down my experiences, I've created a record of moments that might have otherwise faded. This has helped me look back and see patterns or recurring themes that reveal God's presence and guidance in my life.

In my journal, I include not only the major events and obvious signs but also the subtle nudges and small coincidences. At the end of each week, I take time to review these entries, asking myself if I feel a deeper meaning emerging. Sometimes, it's only after reflecting that I realize how interconnected these moments are—like puzzle pieces forming a larger picture.

Reflection deepens my understanding of these experiences. After a particularly significant moment, I set aside time for quiet prayer, asking God to help me understand His message. I've also found it helpful to bring these moments to my spiritual community, sharing them with others who can offer their insights. Often, a friend's perspective can shed light on an aspect I hadn't considered, making me more aware of how God is speaking to me.

As I've journeyed through life, I've learned that divine signs are not always grand revelations; more often, they are small moments of grace that remind us of God's enduring love. Each sign, whether a major event or a quiet nudge, is a reminder that we are not alone—that God is walking with us, guiding us, and speaking to us in ways both big and small.

Through journaling, reflecting, and embracing the moments that feel like more than coincidence, we can strengthen our connection with the divine. I hope that sharing these experiences encourages others to recognize the signs in their own lives, to trust in the quiet whispers and to open their hearts to the presence of God.

For me, every moment, every nudge, is woven into the fabric of faith, creating a life rich with purpose, connection, and a profound sense of divine love. And while life's path may be uncertain, I know that if I stay attuned, God's signs will continue to light the way, one step at a time.

24

Chapter 5
The Power of Prayer and Meditation

Prayer has guided human life through the centuries, holding spiritual meaning across cultures, faiths, and beliefs. For countless people, including myself, prayer is far more than a ritual; it is a lifeline to something greater, a direct way to reach out to God. In prayer, we open our hearts, seek guidance, find comfort, and express gratitude. These moments allow us to feel supported and lifted up, even when challenges arise.

Across history, prayer has shaped humanity's relationship with the divine in unique ways. In Christianity, prayer is a core part of faith—a way to connect with God through praise, repentance, and asking for help. In Islam, prayer is embedded in daily life, with five dedicated times each day that allow believers to center themselves in their faith and devotion to Allah. In Hinduism and Buddhism, prayer and meditation are sacred practices that deepen self-awareness and offer moments of peace to the mind and spirit. Judaism sees prayer as an ongoing conversation with God, infused with commitments to justice, compassion, and community. Each of these traditions shows how prayer has given meaning and comfort across time, revealing its ability to reach beyond religious boundaries and bring us closer to the divine.

In my own life, prayer has been a constant support, something I turn to for reassurance and direction, especially in times of uncertainty. It fills me with a deep sense of confidence that God is walking alongside me, reminding me I am never alone in any endeavor or difficulty. Every night before bed, I take time to pray. This practice is more than a routine; it's a personal moment where I release the day's worries, place my trust in God, and rest in the peace that comes from knowing He is always near.

One night, as I was preparing for bed, I found myself anxious about the next chapter in my life's journey. I had decided to write my first book on business, and although I felt excited, I was overwhelmed by the unknowns of the process. I didn't know where to begin or how to structure the book in a way that would benefit others. In that moment, I turned to prayer, speaking softly to God, careful not to disturb anyone, including my little Yorkie, who lay peacefully by my side. I asked God to show me the way, to guide my steps, and to fill me with the wisdom and clarity I lacked.

What happened next felt almost miraculous. Over the following days, my mind opened to ideas and insights that seemed to come from beyond myself. I knew God had heard my prayer that He was guiding me through each step of the process. I had to make a few changes along the way, but the heart of the book took shape with His help. Today, that book remains one of my proudest achievements, not just for its content but because it represents the power of prayer in my life. This experience showed me that prayer is more than a way to ask for help—it is a real, active conversation with God that can inspire and empower us to reach our goals.

In addition to this, I have witnessed moments of answered prayer in ways that felt nearly miraculous, showing me that prayer is not only a way to grow but also a way for God to step in and change the course of events. One experience I will never forget involved former President Donald J. Trump, a man for whom I regularly pray. During his time in office, there was an assassination attempt—a bullet that missed his head by mere inches. When I heard about it, I felt strongly that God's hand had intervened, protecting him in a way beyond ordinary explanation. Some in the press even called it "divine intervention," and I couldn't agree more. This moment deepened my faith in prayer and reminded me that God has a plan, even when we may not understand every detail.

This experience inspired me to name this book *Divine Intervention*, as it reflects my belief that God acts in our lives in ways we might never fully understand. Praying for someone in a position of great influence, I felt a unique responsibility to intercede for someone who could affect the future of the country. Through this prayer, I found a stronger sense of purpose and a renewed trust that God is indeed present, working through those He has placed in leadership. I continue to pray for Trump's guidance, resilience, and strength, and I often wonder if God chose him to protect the values and ideals that America holds dear.

To me, prayer is a simple, honest conversation with God. There are no formalities, no rules—just an open exchange of thoughts and feelings from my spirit to His. In times of struggle, prayer offers a comfort that I have not found anywhere else. When I pray, I feel seen and understood by God, confident that He listens to me, understands my worries, and, in His own time, will provide the answers I seek. This trust has become a steady guide, especially in challenging times when I feel uncertain or vulnerable.

I also find that prayer creates a deep sense of gratitude. At the end of each prayer, I always take a moment to thank God. I thank Him not only for the good but also for the challenges, knowing that each difficulty brings me closer to His purpose. I also express gratitude for the animals that have brought love and joy into my life, especially my little Yorkie. I believe that animals have souls just as humans do; they, too, are part of God's creation, teaching us about loyalty, kindness, and compassion. These moments of thanksgiving are often the most meaningful parts of my prayer, filling my heart with peace and reassurance.

Though I do not practice meditation myself, I see how it could complement prayer by calming the mind and creating space to hear God's voice more clearly. Meditation can be a way to quiet the mind, focusing on God's presence in a gentle and undistracted way. Some people find meditation beneficial as a space for deep breathing and centering themselves, creating a peaceful mindset.

One simple meditation practice is to close your eyes, take slow, deep breaths, and visualize a light filling your heart and radiating outward. This light can represent God's love, a reminder that His presence is always with you. Sitting in silence, even for just a few minutes, can bring a sense of clarity and peace that supports a spiritual connection to the divine. In this way, meditation can help people feel calm, supported, and grounded, helping them to reconnect with their faith and purpose.

Through the years, I've come to understand that prayer is not just a source of comfort—it is a way to open ourselves to God's help in our lives. When I pray, I ask for wisdom and allow God to guide me down paths I might not have seen on my own. Prayer has the ability to transform our circumstances, bring about opportunities that seemed impossible, and create change in ways that are hard to explain.

One of the most humbling lessons in prayer has been accepting that God's answers may not always match my requests. There have been times when I prayed for something specific, only to find that God had a different plan that brought me even greater blessings than I had imagined. Through prayer, I have learned to let go, and to trust that God's timing and purpose are more profound than my own. This willingness to trust is not always easy; it calls for patience, faith, and an openness to accept what may come. But in that surrender, I have found peace that comes from knowing God is in control, guiding me in ways I might not understand right away.

Prayer and meditation can be profoundly healing, not just physically but also emotionally and spiritually. There have been times when prayer has soothed my soul in moments of sorrow, restoring my hope and reminding me that God is always present. When we open our hearts in prayer, we invite divine love and compassion into our lives, allowing God's presence to heal our inner wounds. I have come to see prayer as a gentle balm that eases life's hardships, bringing peace to those who are burdened.

In closing, prayer and meditation are practices that bring us closer to the divine, reminding us that we are part of something greater than ourselves. Through prayer, we find strength, hope, and guidance—a way to invite

God into our lives in moments of need and gratitude alike. Whether we are seeking comfort, clarity, or a connection to God, prayer and meditation provide a pathway to inner peace and divine support. For me, prayer has been a source of comfort and direction, carrying me through both the challenges and blessings of life.

Chapter 6
Love as a Divine Force

Love is often regarded as one of the most profound and transformative forces in the human experience. It reaches beyond individual boundaries, unites families, builds communities, and fosters resilience in the face of life's greatest challenges. In its deepest and most spiritual form, love transcends human limitations, offering a glimpse into something far greater than ourselves. This divine love, which I have come to experience in my own life, acts as a bridge between the earthly and the sacred, reminding us that we are connected to something infinitely larger and more beautiful than we might fully understand.

Divine love, unlike human love, is unconditional and limitless. It is a love that exists beyond our frailties and mistakes, a love that doesn't depend on our actions, worthiness, or achievements. It is simply there— boundless, compassionate, and forgiving. I believe that this divine love is woven into the fabric of our being, a force that quietly shapes our souls and connects us to God and to each other. Reflecting on this form of love, I often find myself humbled by its sheer immensity and the sense of peace it brings.

Many religious teachings speak of this kind of love as the purest and most essential expression of divinity. In Christianity, for instance, this concept of divine love is often referred to as "agape," an unconditional love that God has for humanity. This love is not contingent on our actions; rather, it is freely given, encompassing all of humanity. In 1 John 4:8, we read, "Whoever does not love does not know God, because God is love." This passage reflects a powerful truth: to truly understand God, we must seek to understand and embody this kind of love ourselves.

Similarly, in Buddhism, divine love is known as *metta*, or loving-kindness. This practice encourages us to cultivate compassion and goodwill for all beings, transcending self-interest. The Dalai Lama, a revered Buddhist figure, often emphasizes that genuine compassion and loving-kindness are the foundation of a peaceful and harmonious society. His words remind me that to love others deeply and selflessly is not only to enrich their lives but also to find a profound sense of happiness within ourselves.

Islam, too, embraces the concept of divine love through Allah's boundless mercy and compassion. The Quran speaks of Allah's love as a guiding force that is merciful, forgiving, and unconditional. In Surah Al-Baqarah (2:165), it is said that "Allah is the Most Merciful, the Most Compassionate," inviting followers to understand that the nature of divine love is one of endless mercy and grace. Reflecting on these teachings from various faiths, I see that divine love is a universal concept that transcends the boundaries of culture and belief, revealing a pathway to unity, compassion, and understanding.

As I have grown older, I have come to witness the powerful impact that divine love has on human relationships. When we allow this kind of love to guide our interactions, we create spaces for healing, growth, and transformation. I have seen relationships mended, friendships deepened, and families strengthened by the presence of divine love—a force that asks us to act with understanding, empathy, and patience.

One of the most beautiful aspects of divine love is its ability to heal old wounds and to create new beginnings. Relationships are often strained by misunderstandings, by words spoken in anger, or by moments of neglect. Yet when we approach these situations with an open heart, willing to forgive and to be vulnerable, divine love steps in, offering a way forward. I have seen this happen in my own life, especially with people who are close to me. In moments where we could have chosen to hold onto grudges or to distance ourselves, we instead chose love—choosing to listen, to apologize, and to forgive. Through these choices, I have witnessed relationships become even stronger than they were before.

I often think of families and how divine love can create an environment where each member feels safe, valued, and understood. In families rooted in divine love, children learn important life lessons about kindness, empathy, and compassion. They learn to support one another in times of difficulty and to celebrate each other's successes, creating bonds that endure through the years. Divine love within a family builds a foundation of mutual respect and shared values, allowing each individual to grow into their fullest self, knowing they are deeply loved.

Communities, too, are transformed by divine love. When people come together with a shared commitment to help each other, they create spaces of belonging and warmth. I am reminded of the civil rights movement, led by leaders like Martin Luther King Jr., who emphasized love as a driving force for social justice and change. He advocated for nonviolent resistance, believing that love could overcome hatred and bridge the divides of race and class. This commitment to divine love inspired millions, showing the world that love—when expressed genuinely and courageously—can change the course of history.

The power of divine love to transform lives is a reality I have seen time and again. Through moments of reconciliation, acts of kindness, and small gestures of care, love has the ability to change our lives in ways we might never have expected.

One story that comes to mind involves two siblings who had been estranged for many years. Their relationship had suffered from misunderstandings and unresolved pain that neither one felt they could face. But when their mother became ill, they found themselves caring for her together. In those quiet moments by her bedside, they began to talk, opening up about their past hurts. One sibling apologized, expressing regret for the words left unsaid and the misunderstandings that had divided them. This simple act of vulnerability and love allowed them to heal together, rediscovering the bond they shared. The divine love that touched their relationship restored it, reminding me that even the deepest wounds can be healed when approached with love.

Another inspiring example of divine love comes from a group of volunteers who dedicated their time to helping the homeless in their community during the winter. They organized food drives and clothing donations, but they also took the time to sit with the people they served, listening to their stories and offering companionship. For many of the volunteers, these interactions were transformative. They came to see the people they were helping as not just strangers but as friends, worthy of love and compassion. Through this experience, the volunteers felt enriched and uplifted, realizing that acts of kindness rooted in divine love create connections that surpass any social or economic divide.

Expressing divine love in daily life can be both a challenge and a joy. It calls us to open our hearts, to practice patience, and to engage with others in ways that are kind and generous. While love is a feeling, it is also an action—one we can cultivate intentionally through simple practices that strengthen our connection to others.

One of the most meaningful practices in my life is expressing gratitude. Each day, I take a few moments to reflect on the blessings around me, whether it is a kind gesture from a friend, a quiet walk in nature, or the warmth of my little Yorkie lying by my side. These moments of gratitude remind me of the beauty in everyday life, helping me to focus on the good rather than dwell on the challenges.

Acts of kindness are another way to bring divine love into our lives. I often make it a goal to do something kind each day, no matter how small. Sometimes, it's helping a stranger, calling a loved one, or leaving a thoughtful note for someone who might need encouragement. These gestures, though simple, carry a power that we may never fully see, touching others in ways we may never know.

I have also found that practicing mindful listening is a profound way to show love. When someone speaks to us, giving them our full attention without interrupting or planning our response shows respect. It lets them know that we truly care about what they have to say. This practice, though small, can deepen our relationships, creating connections that are genuine and filled with understanding.

Forgiveness, too, is an essential part of divine love. In life, we inevitably encounter situations where we are hurt by others or where we hurt ourselves through mistakes. Writing letters of forgiveness—whether to someone else or to ourselves—has been a deeply healing practice for me. Even if these letters are never sent, they serve as a release, a way of letting go of the pain that might otherwise weigh us down.

Meditating on love has also become a cherished practice. I sometimes dedicate a few minutes to sitting quietly, closing my eyes, and visualizing a light of love filling my heart and radiating outward. I imagine this light surrounding not only those I hold dear but also strangers, people I have yet to meet, and even those with whom I might have disagreements. This meditation fills me with a sense of peace, reminding me that we are all connected by the same love that flows from God.

As I reflect on the nature of divine love, I am reminded that it is indeed a force unlike any other. It shapes our lives in profound ways, affecting our relationships, communities, and the very essence of who we are. When we embrace divine love, we open ourselves to a deeper understanding of life, one that is filled with compassion, forgiveness, and unity.

Love, when given freely and without expectation, has the power to heal old wounds, create new connections, and bring about change that transcends anything we might achieve on our own. Divine love is a gift, one that teaches us to see beyond ourselves and to recognize the beauty and worth in every person we encounter. As we navigate the complexities of life, may we hold onto this love, knowing that it is the thread that binds us to God and to each other.

In all the ways we express love—whether through a kind word, a listening ear, or a gentle act of forgiveness—we bring a little more light into the world. And in doing so, we become vessels of divine love, guided by a force that is as infinite as it is beautiful. Love is what makes us human, and it is love that connects us to the divine, drawing us ever closer to the heart of God.

35

Chapter 7
Community and Support

Community is one of the most profound gifts we are given in life. It is where we find belonging, share our triumphs and struggles, and experience the presence of God in others. When we think about divine intervention—those moments when God's hand seems to touch our lives in ways that are undeniable—it often happens in the context of community. Whether through collective prayer, acts of service, or the quiet support of those who care for us, God often works through the people around us.

I remember a time in my own life when the community became a vessel for divine intervention. A close friend was going through a severe illness. She was not only battling the physical toll of her condition but was also grappling with deep spiritual doubts. A group of us—her friends, family, and members of her church—decided to come together in prayer. Every night, we gathered in her living room, holding hands, our voices uniting as we called out to God for her healing and peace.

It wasn't just the act of praying that made this experience so profound; it was the way we collectively carried her burden. In those moments, I saw divine love in action. As days turned into weeks, something shifted. While her health took time to improve, her spirit was renewed. She often told us later that it was our prayers, our presence, and the shared faith of her community that gave her the strength to endure. In that circle of love, we experienced divine intervention—not just in her healing but in the way we were all drawn closer to God and to each other.

The Bible speaks powerfully to this idea of community as a catalyst for God's work. Hebrews 10:24-25 says, *"And let us consider how we may spur one another on toward love and good deeds, not giving up meeting together, as some are in the habit of doing, but encouraging one another—and all the more as you see the*

Day approaching." When we gather together in faith, we create a space where God's presence can be felt more deeply, where miracles—both great and small—are made possible.

Human beings are designed for connection. In spiritual terms, we have essential needs that are most fully met in the context of community: the need to belong, the need to understand and grow in our faith, the need to have hope, and the need to be equipped for service. These foundational needs are like pillars, supporting our relationship with God and our ability to experience His intervention in our lives.

Belonging is perhaps the most fundamental of these needs. In a community, we find people who know us, love us, and accept us as we are. This sense of belonging mirrors the way God loves us—unconditionally and without reservation. It reminds me of a young man I once knew who had struggled for years with addiction. When he finally joined a faith-based recovery group, he found a community that didn't judge him for his past but instead celebrated every small step he took toward healing. Through their encouragement and accountability, he began to see himself not as broken but as beloved—a child of God.

Hope is another spiritual need that thrives in the community. Life can be isolating and overwhelming, especially during times of hardship. But when we are surrounded by others who share our faith, we are reminded that we are never alone. I recall attending a candlelight vigil for a family that had lost everything in a house fire. The community came together not only to pray but also to provide practical support—clothing, meals, and temporary housing. The love and generosity they experienced became a tangible sign of God's care, restoring their hope even in the midst of tragedy.

In every faith journey, there comes a time when we realize we cannot go it alone. Building supportive networks—relationships with friends, mentors, and fellow believers—is vital for nurturing our faith and staying strong during life's challenges. These networks provide not only emotional support but also spiritual encouragement, helping us to recognize God's hand in our lives.

I've seen the power of supportive networks firsthand in the form of small Bible study groups. One such group I participated in was a lifeline during a particularly difficult season in my life. We met every Thursday evening, gathering in a cozy living room with cups of tea and well-worn Bibles. Each session began with laughter and light conversation, but as we delved into Scripture and shared our personal stories, something profound happened.

There was one evening I'll never forget. A woman in our group broke down in tears, sharing a secret burden she had carried for years. As she spoke, the rest of us leaned in, offering words of comfort, encouragement, and prayer. By the end of the night, she said she felt lighter—as though God had used our group to lift her burden. That evening taught me that supportive networks are not just about companionship; they are about being vessels for God's grace.

Building long-term connections is another crucial aspect of supportive networks. These relationships, cultivated over time, provide a steady foundation that sustains us through life's ups and downs. Long-term connections remind us that we are seen, known, and loved—not only by those around us but also by God.

There is something uniquely powerful about engaging in faith-based communities. Whether it's a church, a prayer group, or a spiritual organization, these communities provide a space where we can grow in faith, serve others, and experience God's presence in profound ways.

One of the most beautiful aspects of faith-based communities is the sense of belonging they offer. Walking into a church on Sunday morning, hearing the hum of voices, the swell of music, and the warm greetings of fellow believers—it feels like coming home. In these spaces, we are reminded that we are part of something larger than ourselves: the body of Christ.

Faith communities also provide countless opportunities for service. Whether it's organizing a food drive, visiting the sick, or mentoring young people, these acts of service not only benefit others but also deepen our own faith. I once participated in a mission trip with my church, traveling to a remote village to help build a school. What struck me most wasn't the physical work we did but the relationships we formed with the villagers. Their gratitude, joy, and resilience were a testament to God's presence in their lives, and I left the experience feeling closer to Him than ever before.

Of all the ways we can experience divine intervention, few are as transformative as serving others. Volunteerism allows us to step outside ourselves, put our faith into action, and become instruments of God's love in the world.

I'll never forget the story of a woman named Clara, a retired teacher who dedicated her time to volunteering at a homeless shelter. One cold winter evening, she sat with a man who had just lost his job and his home. As they talked, she shared her own story of overcoming hardship, and by the end of their conversation, he said her words had given him hope to keep going. Months later, he returned to the shelter, this time as a volunteer himself. He told Clara that her kindness had been a turning point in his life—a moment where he felt God's love reach him through her actions.

Stories like Clara's remind us that when we serve others, we create space for divine intervention. It might be in a small gesture—a kind word, a listening ear—or in larger acts of generosity. Whatever the scale, these moments are opportunities for God to work through us.

Volunteerism also has a way of deepening our own faith. Stepping into situations where we must rely on God's guidance stretches us, teaching us to trust Him more fully. I've experienced this personally during volunteer work with a youth mentorship program. Each time I met with my mentee, I prayed for wisdom to guide her well. Those prayers not only helped me support her but also strengthened my own relationship with God.

Perhaps one of the most moving examples of the power of community is the story of a neighborhood devastated by a natural disaster. After a hurricane tore through their town, leaving homes in ruins, the residents could have succumbed to despair. Instead, they came together. Churches opened their doors to shelter the displaced. Neighbors shared food, water, and supplies. Volunteers arrived from other towns to help with clean-up and rebuilding efforts.

One family, whose home had been completely destroyed, said it was the kindness of their community that gave them the strength to start over. They described how a group of strangers showed up one morning with tools and began repairing their roof. "In those moments," the father said, "we knew we weren't alone. God was with us—through them."

This story illustrates a profound truth: when communities come together in love and service, they become living reflections of God's presence. They remind us that divine intervention often comes not in grand miracles but in the quiet, consistent acts of compassion, we show one another.

As I reflect on the importance of community and support, I am reminded of the countless ways God works through the people around us. Whether it's a friend who offers a listening ear, a church that becomes a second family, or a stranger whose kindness changes our day, community is a gift—a channel through which we experience God's love and grace.

When we invest in building relationships, when we engage in faith-based communities, and when we serve others with open hearts, we create spaces where divine intervention can thrive. And in doing so, we not only bless others but also draw closer to the heart of God.

Let us never underestimate the power of community. It is where faith is nurtured, hope is restored, and love is made tangible. It is where we find God—in the faces of those around us, in the prayers we share, and in the lives we touch. And it is where we are reminded that we are never, ever alone.

Chapter 8
Miracles in Everyday Life

Miracles are often defined as extraordinary events that transcend the universe's natural laws, typically attributed to divine intervention. The concept of a miracle invokes awe, wonder, and amazement, drawing us into a deeper recognition of the divine presence in our world. But how do we truly understand what constitutes a miracle? Is it an event that defies nature, something inexplicable by human understanding? Or is it simply a matter of perspective—of seeing the divine hand in the ordinary moments of our lives?

In the biblical sense, a miracle is God's direct and powerful action. It is often seen as an event that cannot be explained by natural laws or human logic, something that only God, in His sovereignty and power, could bring to pass. Miracles serve as a testament to God's greatness, His ability to intervene in the world, and His deep care for humanity. Whether it's a healing, a nature miracle, or a life-changing event, these acts are intended to reveal God's power, grace, and love.

The Bible provides numerous examples of miracles, some of which have become emblematic of the divine work in the world. From healing miracles like the restoration of sight to the blind to nature miracles such as the parting of the Red Sea to the ultimate miracle of resurrection, these events remind us that God can defy the very laws of nature when He chooses. For instance, when Jesus healed the blind or raised the dead, He demonstrated His authority over both life and death. When He calmed a storm with a word, He proved that He held dominion over nature itself.

Yet, while biblical miracles are the most widely recognized, the definition of a miracle is not confined to extraordinary events alone. Many theologians and philosophers, such as David Hume, have argued that for something to be considered a miracle, it must be a violation of the laws of nature. Hume's perspective suggests that miracles are rare and exceptional, events that occur outside the realm of human experience or expectation. But what if miracles are not just grand occurrences but also small, quiet signs of God's presence that we fail to see in the busyness of our lives?

Today, in a world that is often skeptical of the supernatural, many people still experience what they consider to be miracles—events that defy logical explanations but are deeply meaningful to the individuals who experience them. These modern miracles are not necessarily the dramatic or life-altering events that are written about in Scripture but rather the personal, intimate moments that connect people with the divine in a profound way. A miraculous recovery from an illness, an unexpected positive turn in a dire situation, or even a moment of deep peace in the midst of chaos can be seen as miracles. These occurrences remind us that divine intervention is not limited to biblical times but continues to manifest in our lives today.

Different Interpretations and Examples of Miracles

The concept of miracles can take many forms, both within religious traditions and beyond. Let's explore a few different interpretations of miracles, from their biblical foundations to their modern-day applications.

1. **Biblical Miracles**: The Bible is rich with accounts of miracles that served a variety of purposes. These events often acted as signs of God's power, His authority, and His loving care for His people. Healing miracles, nature miracles, and resurrection miracles are perhaps the most well-known.

    o **Healing Miracles**: In the New Testament, healing miracles performed by Jesus are numerous and varied. From healing the blind to restoring the ability to walk to curing lepers, each healing was an act of compassion and a profound revelation of God's power. One of the most powerful healing miracles is the healing of two blind men who cried out to Jesus for mercy. They were healed immediately when Jesus touched their eyes (Matthew 9:27-31). This miracle restored their physical sight and revealed the spiritual truth that Jesus was the world's Light.

- o **Nature Miracles**: Another well-known type of miracle is that of nature miracles. One of the most dramatic examples is the parting of the Red Sea, where Moses parted the waters with God's guidance to allow the Israelites to escape from Pharaoh's army (Exodus 14:21-22). The calming of the storm by Jesus, when He rebuked the wind and the waves with a simple command, is another striking example (Mark 4:35-41). These miracles demonstrate that God is sovereign over nature and nothing is beyond His control.

- o **Resurrection Miracles**: The resurrection of Jesus, one of the cornerstones of the Christian faith, is perhaps the ultimate miracle. When Jesus raised Lazarus from the dead (John 11:38-46), it demonstrated His power over death and foreshadowed His own resurrection. The resurrection of Jesus offers believers the hope of eternal life and confirms His divinity.

2. **Philosophical Perspective**: From a philosophical standpoint, miracles are often seen as violations of natural laws. David Hume's famous definition of miracles suggests that a miracle is an event that exceeds the natural possibilities of the world. It is something that cannot be explained by science or reason. While Hume's view emphasizes the rarity and exceptional nature of miracles, many modern theologians argue that miracles can be more than just rare occurrences—they can be part of the daily fabric of life, waiting to be recognized and appreciated.

3. **Modern Interpretations**: In the modern world, many people continue to experience what they believe are miracles, although they may not necessarily align with the biblical or philosophical definitions. For instance, some might consider miraculous a sudden, unexplained recovery from a terminal illness. Others may see miracles in the form of extraordinary coincidences or divine timing—when an event occurs at just the right moment to change the course of someone's life. These experiences often defy explanation but leave an indelible mark on the individual's faith and sense of the divine.

Anecdotes and Testimonies

There are countless stories of individuals experiencing miracles in their lives. These personal accounts help us see the divine at work in the world today and remind us that miracles are not confined to ancient times or to the pages of Scripture.

1. **Greg Thomas's Healing**: Greg Thomas was diagnosed with terminal cancer. His prognosis was grim, and doctors had given him little hope for survival. But instead of succumbing to despair, Greg found solace in an unusual place: he dedicated his time to restoring an old church. As he worked tirelessly, pouring his energy into the renovation, something remarkable began to happen. His health, which had been rapidly declining, began to improve. Over time, Greg made a full recovery, a recovery that defied medical logic. Greg attributes his healing to divine intervention, believing that God worked in his body as he worked on the church. This testimony serves as a reminder that God's miracles often come in unexpected forms and that faith and service can be powerful conduits for divine intervention.

2. **Morgan Lake's Escape**: Morgan Lake's story is one that defies the laws of nature. One evening, while driving, Morgan was struck by a truck and pushed off a bridge into icy waters. As her car sank, she felt an unseen force guiding her to safety. She

managed to escape just in time, emerging from the icy water, bruised but alive. Morgan believes her survival was a miracle—a clear instance of God's hand intervening to save her life. Her testimony speaks to the belief that miracles are not always grand spectacles but can be deeply personal, life-saving moments when God steps in to protect us.

3. **Vesna Vulovic's Fall**: One of the most miraculous survival stories of the 20th century involves Vesna Vulovic, a flight attendant who survived a fall from 33,000 feet after her plane exploded mid-air. Vesna was the only survivor of the crash, and her miraculous survival has been hailed as one of the greatest modern-day miracles. She endured severe injuries but ultimately made a remarkable recovery. Her survival defied all odds and is considered by many to be a testament to divine protection. This incredible story is a powerful reminder that miracles can occur even in the most unlikely and tragic circumstances.

These anecdotes, while different in nature, all share a common thread: the belief that the miraculous is not limited to the past but continues to occur in the lives of everyday people. Miracles, whether they are personal healings, narrow escapes, or extraordinary survivals, show us that God is still at work in the world today.

Recognizing the Ordinary as Extraordinary

As we reflect on the stories above, it's easy to see miracles as rare, life-altering events. However, what if we learned to recognize the extraordinary in everyday life? What if the simple acts of kindness, moments of peace, and even the small blessings we often take for granted were, in fact, miracles?

1. **Mindfulness Practices**: One way to cultivate this awareness is through mindfulness practices. Mindfulness encourages us to slow down and become fully present in the moment. Whether enjoying a walk in nature, savoring a meal, or having a

conversation with a loved one, mindfulness helps us recognize that every moment is a gift—a miracle in itself. When we cultivate mindfulness, we begin to see the divine in the everyday occurrences that we might otherwise overlook.

2. **Gratitude Journaling**: Gratitude journaling is another powerful practice for recognizing the extraordinary in the ordinary. By taking time each day to reflect on the things we are grateful for—no matter how small—we train our minds to see blessings all around us. Keeping a gratitude journal allows us to track the miracles, big and small, that happen each day. It shifts our perspective, turning mundane tasks into moments of appreciation for the life we have.

3. **Spiritual Reflection**: Spiritual reflection, whether through prayer, meditation, or quiet contemplation, is another way to recognize God's presence in the ordinary. Taking time to reflect on the blessings of the day helps us see how God is at work in our lives, even in the most ordinary moments. This spiritual discipline allows us to slow down, to listen, and to feel God's presence guiding us in every aspect of life.

4. **Community Engagement**: Engaging with others in community service or acts of kindness can also help us see the miracles in our daily lives. When we reach out to others, when we offer help to someone in need, we become instruments of God's grace. These acts of kindness, though simple, can transform lives, and in doing so, we become part of the miracle.

Cultivating an Attitude of Gratitude

Recognizing miracles requires intentionality, and one of the most powerful ways to do this is by cultivating an attitude of gratitude. Gratitude opens our hearts to the divine and helps us see the abundance in our lives rather than focusing on what we lack.

1. **Daily Affirmations**: Begin each day with positive affirmations focused on gratitude. This practice sets a tone of appreciation for the day ahead. By consciously choosing to focus on what we are thankful for, we invite more blessings into our lives.

2. **Gratitude Challenges**: Engaging in gratitude challenges is another effective way to foster appreciation. For instance, challenge yourself to thank someone new every day or to share three things you are grateful for at dinner. These small exercises can help rewire your brain to see the positive in every situation.

3. **Mindful Appreciation**: Taking moments throughout the day to pause and appreciate your surroundings—whether it's a beautiful sunset, the smell of fresh flowers, or the warmth of a cup of coffee—can bring you back to the present moment and remind you of the miracles in your life.

4. **Acts of Kindness**: Engaging in random acts of kindness not only benefits others but also enhances our own sense of gratitude. When we give without expecting anything in return, we create space for miracles to unfold.

5. **Reflective Meditation**: Spend time reflecting on specific moments in your life where you felt blessed or experienced something miraculous. Reflecting on these moments can deepen your appreciation for life's gifts and remind you of the divine presence that surrounds you.

6. **Sharing Stories**: Finally, share your stories of miracles with others. Whether through conversation or writing, sharing these personal testimonies can inspire others to recognize the miracles in their own lives.

Conclusion

In conclusion, recognizing miracles requires both awareness and intention. It requires a shift in perspective—a willingness to see the divine hand at work in both the extraordinary and the ordinary. By understanding what constitutes a miracle, sharing personal testimonies, seeing the extraordinary within the ordinary, and cultivating gratitude, we can enrich our lives with a deeper appreciation for the divine presence woven through every moment. Miracles are not confined to the pages of Scripture or the great events of history. They are all around us, waiting to be recognized, cherished, and celebrated.

Chapter 9
Historical Examples of Divine Intervention

Divine intervention has often been credited for shaping pivotal moments in history and the lives of individuals who influenced the course of society. In this chapter, we will explore the stories of two historical figures—George Washington and Eric Liddell—whose lives were marked by extraordinary events they attributed to the hand of Providence. These case studies will illuminate the impact of faith, resilience, and divine guidance, offering timeless lessons for modern life.

George Washington: A Life Guided by Providence

Background

George Washington (1732–1799), the first President of the United States, is celebrated as a leader of vision and integrity. Born into a planter family in Virginia, Washington's early life was shaped by a sense of duty and an innate ability to lead. His journey—from a young surveyor to Commander-in-Chief of the Continental Army and ultimately the leader of a new nation—was fraught with challenges that he navigated with steadfast faith. Many of these trials were punctuated by events he believed to be acts of divine intervention.

Key Events of Divine Intervention

The French and Indian War (1754–1763): Washington's military career began during the French and Indian War, where his experiences showcased the early signs of what he perceived as divine protection. In 1755, during the Battle of Monongahela, Washington served as an aide-de-camp to British General Edward Braddock. When the British forces were ambushed by a coalition of French troops and their Native American allies, chaos ensued. Despite being a prime target—four bullets pierced his coat, and two horses were shot from under him—

Washington emerged unharmed. This improbable survival led him to write to his brother, "By the all-powerful dispensation of Providence, I have been protected beyond all human probability or expectation." This event was seen by many as a sign of his divine calling.

The American Revolution (1775–1783): Washington's leadership during the Revolutionary War was another period filled with moments he attributed to divine intervention. One of the most striking examples was the miraculous escape of his army after the Battle of Long Island in 1776. Trapped by British forces, Washington's troops seemed doomed to destruction. However, under the cover of an unusual fog that shrouded their movements, his army successfully crossed the East River to Manhattan. Many saw this unexpected natural phenomenon as an act of God preserving the Continental Army.

The Crossing of the Delaware (1776): One of the most iconic moments of the Revolution occurred on Christmas night in 1776, when Washington led his troops across the icy Delaware River to launch a surprise attack on Hessian forces in Trenton. This bold maneuver, conducted under extreme weather conditions, resulted in a decisive victory that reinvigorated American morale. Washington's belief in divine guidance was evident as he consistently emphasized the importance of faith and prayer in rallying his troops.

Legacy of Divine Intervention

Throughout his life, Washington frequently referenced Providence in his speeches and writings. In his inaugural address as President, he acknowledged, "No people can be bound to acknowledge and adore the Invisible Hand which conducts the affairs of men more than the people of the United States." His unwavering faith shaped his vision for America, emphasizing principles of liberty, justice, and reliance on divine guidance. Washington's story shows how faith in divine intervention can inspire resilience and shape leadership.

Eric Liddell: The Olympian Missionary

Background

Eric Henry Liddell (1902–1945) was a Scottish athlete and devout Christian whose life embodied the principles of faith and sacrifice. Born in China to missionary parents, Liddell's upbringing instilled in him a deep commitment to serving God. He rose to international fame as an Olympic gold medalist before dedicating his life to missionary work, demonstrating an unwavering faith that inspired millions.

Key Events of Divine Intervention

1924 Paris Olympics: Liddell's defining moment came during the 1924 Olympics, where his commitment to his faith took center stage. Scheduled to compete in the 100 meters, Liddell discovered that the heats would take place on a Sunday. Due to his belief in observing the Sabbath, he refused to participate despite immense pressure from officials and public expectations. Instead, he competed in the 400 meters, a race he had not trained for extensively. Against all odds, Liddell not only won but also set a new world record. He later attributed his success to God's favor, famously stating, "When I run, I feel His pleasure."

Missionary Work in China: Liddell returned to China to serve as a missionary after his Olympic triumph. He taught at an Anglo-Chinese school and used sports as a tool to connect with students while sharing the Gospel. His work reflected his belief in living a life of service, guided by divine purpose. Despite increasing tensions in China during the 1930s, Liddell remained steadfast in his mission, often citing his faith as the source of his courage.

Internment During World War II: In 1943, Liddell was interned in the Weihsien Internment Camp by Japanese forces. Conditions in the camp were harsh, but Liddell's faith never wavered. He organized educational activities, led prayer groups, and supported fellow prisoners spiritually. His selflessness and unwavering hope became a beacon of light in the camp. Even as his health declined due to an undiagnosed brain tumor,

Liddell continued to serve others until he died in 1945. His final words, "It's complete surrender," personified his faith and trust in God's plan.

Legacy of Divine Intervention

Eric Liddell's life has been immortalized in various forms, most notably in the film *Chariots of Fire*. His story exemplifies how faith can guide individuals to make courageous decisions and endure hardship. Liddell's unwavering belief in divine intervention inspired countless people to live with integrity and purpose.

Andrew Jackson: A Controversial Presidency and Indian Removal

Background

Andrew Jackson (1767–1845), the seventh President of the United States, served from 1829 to 1837. He rose from humble beginnings to become a military hero and a prominent political figure known for his populist approach and strong leadership style. Jackson's presidency is marked by significant events, particularly his controversial policies regarding Native American removal, which had lasting impacts on indigenous communities.

Key Events of Divine Intervention

1835 Circular to the Cherokee Tribe: In a circular addressed to the Cherokee people, Jackson laid out his rationale for their removal from Georgia. He employed paternalistic and threatening language, asserting that their survival depended on relocating westward. He stated, "Circumstances that cannot be controlled… render it impossible that you can flourish in the midst of a civilized community." This message reflected his belief that divine circumstances necessitated their removal for their own good.

Trail of Tears: The culmination of Jackson's Indian removal policy led to the Trail of Tears, where thousands of Cherokees were forcibly relocated to Oklahoma. This tragic journey resulted in immense suffering and death, with nearly a quarter of the Cherokee population perishing due to starvation, illness, and exposure during the trek. Jackson's insistence on removal despite Supreme Court rulings against it demonstrated his commitment to what he perceived as a divinely ordained mission to expand American territory.

Legacy of Divine Intervention

Jackson's presidency was characterized by his belief in his role as a leader chosen to fulfill a divine purpose for America. His actions toward Native Americans have been widely criticized as morally reprehensible, yet he framed them as necessary for progress and civilization. The consequences of his policies continue to resonate in discussions about justice and human rights in American history.

Theodore Roosevelt: The Progressive Reformer

Background

Theodore Roosevelt (1858–1919), the 26th President of the United States, served from 1901 to 1909. Known for his robust personality and progressive policies, Roosevelt was a driving force behind significant reforms aimed at curbing corporate power and promoting social justice. His presidency marked a transformative period in American politics, characterized by an aggressive approach to domestic policy and international diplomacy.

Key Events of Divine Intervention

1912 Presidential Campaign: After serving two terms as president, Roosevelt sought a third term in 1912 under the Progressive Party banner after feeling that his successor, William Howard Taft, had strayed from progressive ideals. His campaign emphasized social justice, labor rights, and environmental conservation. Roosevelt's determination was fueled by a belief in his mission to protect the American people from corporate greed and political corruption 12.

The New Nationalism Speech: In a pivotal speech delivered during the campaign, Roosevelt articulated his vision for America's future, emphasizing the need for government intervention to ensure fairness and equality. He argued that "the welfare of each of us is dependent fundamentally upon the welfare of all of us," invoking a sense of collective responsibility that resonated with many Americans 3. This speech underscored his belief in a higher purpose guiding his reform efforts.

Legacy of Divine Intervention

Roosevelt's legacy is one of dynamic leadership and significant reform. He championed conservation efforts, established national parks, and fought against monopolies through antitrust legislation. His belief in a divinely inspired duty to improve society shaped modern American governance and left an indelible mark on the nation's trajectory toward progressivism.

Franklin Delano Roosevelt: The Architect of the New Deal

Background

Franklin Delano Roosevelt (1882–1945), the 32nd President of the United States, served from 1933 until his death in 1945. He assumed office during the Great Depression, a time of unprecedented economic hardship. Roosevelt's leadership style and policies transformed the role of the federal government in American life, emphasizing direct intervention to address social and economic issues.

Key Events of Divine Intervention

Inaugural Address, March 4, 1933: Roosevelt's first inaugural address is famously remembered for his declaration that "the only thing we have to fear is fear itself." This statement aimed to reassure a nation in turmoil and reflected his belief that strong leadership could guide the country through its crises. He pledged a "new deal" for the American people, indicating a commitment to proactive governance during dire times. His confidence was rooted in a conviction that he was chosen to lead the nation through its darkest hour.

The New Deal Programs: The New Deal encompassed a series of programs and reforms aimed at economic recovery and social welfare. Initiatives such as the Civilian Conservation Corps (CCC) and the Works Progress Administration (WPA) were established to provide jobs and infrastructure improvements. Roosevelt viewed these efforts as not merely governmental responses but as a moral obligation to help citizens in need, believing that divine providence guided his actions to restore hope and stability to America.

Legacy of Divine Intervention

Roosevelt's presidency fundamentally reshaped American governance, establishing a precedent for federal involvement in economic and social affairs. His belief in divine guidance fueled his resolve to implement sweeping reforms that addressed the needs of millions suffering from the Great Depression. The New Deal's legacy continues to influence American policy and public expectations regarding government responsibility.

Harry Truman: The Decision Maker in Post-War America

Background

Harry S. Truman (1884–1972), the 33rd President of the United States, served from 1945 to 1953. He assumed office after Roosevelt's death and faced significant challenges during a transformative period in world history, including the conclusion of World War II and the beginning of the Cold War. Truman is known for his decisive leadership style and commitment to international diplomacy.

Key Events of Divine Intervention

The Truman Doctrine, 1947: In response to growing tensions with the Soviet Union, Truman articulated a foreign policy strategy known as the Truman Doctrine. This doctrine asserted that it was America's responsibility to support free peoples resisting subjugation by armed minorities or outside pressures. Truman framed this commitment as not only a strategic necessity but also a moral imperative, suggesting that divine principles guided his decision to protect democracy worldwide.

Korean War Decisions, 1950: During the Korean War, Truman faced critical decisions regarding military intervention. His choice to commit U.S. forces without congressional approval was driven by a belief in containing communism as part of a broader divine mission to promote freedom and democracy globally. Truman famously stated, "The buck stops here," indicating his acceptance of responsibility for these monumental decisions, which he believed were aligned with moral duty.

Legacy of Divine Intervention

Truman's presidency is marked by significant foreign policy decisions that shaped post-war America and its role on the global stage. His belief in moral responsibility and divine guidance influenced his approach to international relations, particularly in confronting communism. Truman's legacy includes establishing key doctrines that defined U.S. foreign policy for decades, emphasizing America's role as a defender of democracy.

Gerald Ford: The Reluctant Leader in a Time of Transition

Background

Gerald Ford (1913–2006), the 38th President of the United States, served from 1974 to 1977. He assumed the presidency in the wake of Richard Nixon's resignation due to the Watergate scandal, making him the first president to ascend from the vice presidency without being elected.

Ford's presidency was marked by efforts to restore public trust in government and navigate the nation through economic challenges.

Key Events of Divine Intervention

Signing of the Tax Reduction Act, 1975: In March 1975, Ford reluctantly signed the Tax Reduction Act, which called for a $22.8 billion tax cut aimed at stimulating the struggling economy. Despite his initial opposition to the bill, he recognized the necessity of action to alleviate the economic hardship faced by millions of Americans. In his address, he expressed a belief that such measures were vital for restoring hope and stability in a nation grappling with recession and inflation, reflecting his sense of duty to serve the American people during turbulent times.

Operation Babylift and Evacuations: As South Vietnam fell to communist forces in April 1975, Ford ordered emergency evacuations of U.S. personnel and South Vietnamese allies. This included Operation Babylift, which aimed to evacuate thousands of orphans from Vietnam. Ford viewed these actions as a moral obligation, believing that it was his responsibility to protect those who had supported American efforts during the war. His leadership during this crisis was guided by a conviction that divine providence compelled him to act in defense of vulnerable populations.

Legacy of Divine Intervention

Ford's presidency is often characterized as a period of healing for a nation recovering from scandal and war. His belief in moral responsibility influenced his decisions, particularly regarding economic recovery and humanitarian efforts. While his presidency faced challenges, including high inflation and unemployment, Ford's commitment to restoring trust in government and addressing pressing issues left a lasting impact on American politics.

Ronald Reagan: The Great Communicator and Conservative Icon

Background

Ronald Reagan (1911–2004), the 40th President of the United States, served from 1981 to 1989. A former actor and California governor, Reagan is celebrated for his charismatic leadership style and significant influence on conservative politics. His presidency marked a shift toward deregulation, tax cuts, and a strong anti-communist stance during the Cold War.

Key Events of Divine Intervention

Inaugural Address, January 20, 1981: Reagan's inaugural address emphasized themes of renewal and hope for America. He stated, "In this present crisis, government is not the solution to our problem; government is the problem." This declaration reflected his belief in limited government intervention and resonated with many Americans seeking change after years of perceived governmental overreach. Reagan's optimistic vision for America was underscored by his faith in divine guidance, leading the nation toward prosperity.

The Cold War Strategy: Throughout his presidency, Reagan adopted a firm stance against communism, famously dubbing the Soviet Union as the "Evil Empire." His administration's policies aimed at rolling back Soviet influence included increased military spending and support for anti-communist movements worldwide. Reagan believed that America had a divine mission to promote freedom and democracy globally, viewing his efforts as part of a larger struggle between good and evil. His faith played a crucial role in shaping his foreign policy decisions during this critical period.

Legacy of Divine Intervention

Reagan's presidency is often credited with revitalizing conservative politics and reshaping American identity during the late 20th century. His belief in divine providence influenced both domestic policies and international relations, particularly regarding the Cold War. Reagan's legacy includes significant tax reforms, a focus on deregulation, and an enduring impact on conservative ideology that continues to resonate in American politics today.

Bill Clinton: A Presidency of Economic Prosperity and Political Challenges

Background

Bill Clinton (1946–), the 42nd President of the United States, served from 1993 to 2001. His presidency is often characterized by economic prosperity, welfare reform, and significant political challenges, including impeachment. Clinton's ability to navigate complex political landscapes and appeal to a broad electorate contributed to his popularity during his two terms in office.

Key Events of Divine Intervention

1996 State of the Union Address: In his annual address delivered on January 23, 1996, Clinton famously declared, "The era of big government is over." This statement reflected his shift towards centrist policies and a commitment to welfare reform. He emphasized the importance of personal responsibility while advocating for government support in areas like education and health care, suggesting a belief that divine guidance was steering the country towards a more balanced approach to governance.

Re-election Campaign: In the 1996 presidential election, Clinton faced Republican nominee Bob Dole. His campaign focused on economic achievements, including job creation and budget surpluses. Clinton's ability to connect with voters on issues that mattered to them—such as healthcare and education—was seen as a demonstration of his leadership qualities. His re-election victory with approximately 70% of the electoral vote underscored his effectiveness in navigating the political landscape and resonating with the American public.

Legacy of Divine Intervention

Clinton's presidency is marked by significant economic growth and the implementation of key policies such as the North American Free Trade Agreement (NAFTA) and welfare reform through the Personal Responsibility and Work Opportunity Reconciliation Act. His administration's focus on centrist policies aimed at bridging partisan divides reflects a belief in the necessity of collaboration for national progress. Despite facing impeachment proceedings in 1998, Clinton's ability to maintain public support highlights his complex legacy as a leader who navigated both triumphs and tribulations.

Donald J. Trump: The Polarizing Figure of Modern Politics

Background

Donald J. Trump (1946–), the 45th President of the United States, served from January 20, 2017, to January 20, 2021. A businessman and television personality prior to his presidency, Trump's tenure was characterized by significant policy changes, controversial rhetoric, and a highly polarized political environment. His approach to governance emphasized nationalism and populism, appealing to a base that felt marginalized by traditional politics.

Key Events of Divine Intervention

Inaugural Address, January 20, 2017: In his inaugural address, Trump proclaimed a vision for America that centered on putting "America First." He emphasized themes of nationalism and economic protectionism while criticizing previous administrations for neglecting American workers. Trump's assertion that he was chosen to restore greatness resonated with many supporters who viewed his election as a form of divine intervention in American politics.

Tax Cuts and Jobs Act, December 2017: One of Trump's signature legislative achievements was the passage of the Tax Cuts and Jobs Act.

This legislation aimed to reduce taxes for individuals and corporations significantly. Trump framed these tax cuts as essential for stimulating economic growth and creating jobs, believing that they would lead to prosperity for all Americans. He often referred to this act as part of fulfilling his promise to revitalize the economy.

Impeachment Proceedings (2019 & 2021): Trump's presidency was marked by two impeachment proceedings—first in December 2019 over allegations related to Ukraine and then again in January 2021 following the Capitol riot on January 6. Throughout these tumultuous events, Trump maintained that he was being persecuted by political opponents who sought to undermine his presidency. He often invoked themes of divine support from his base, framing himself as a defender against what he described as an establishment intent on silencing him.

2020 Presidential Election: The contentious 2020 election saw Trump run for re-election against Joe Biden. After losing the election, Trump made unfounded claims about widespread voter fraud, which culminated in efforts to overturn election results. His refusal to concede and subsequent actions were viewed by many as undermining democratic processes. Trump's rhetoric during this period continued to emphasize a belief that he was fighting for a higher cause, appealing to supporters who felt their values were under attack.

Assassination Attempt in Pennsylvania, July 13, 2024: On July 13, 2024, while speaking at an open-air campaign rally in Butler County, Pennsylvania, Trump survived an assassination attempt when Thomas Matthew Crooks fired eight rounds from an AR-15-style rifle. Trump was shot in the upper right ear but survived the attack. The incident resulted in the death of one audience member and injuries to several others before Crooks was shot and killed by Secret Service agents. This event underscored the heightened risks faced by Trump during his campaign for the Republican nomination in the upcoming presidential election.

Second Assassination Attempt in Florida, September 15, 2024: Just two months later, on September 15, another assassination attempt occurred at Trump's golf course in West Palm Beach. Ryan Wesley Routh was apprehended after being spotted with a rifle aimed at Trump's direction from a distance of several hundred yards. Although Routh did not discharge his weapon, he was charged with attempted murder, among other offenses. This incident highlighted ongoing threats against Trump during his campaign and raised concerns about security measures surrounding public figures.

Threats from Iran: In November 2024, it was reported that Iranian operatives had been directed by the Islamic Revolutionary Guard Corps (IRGC) to surveil and potentially assassinate Trump before the upcoming election. This revelation pointed to international dimensions of threats against him and reinforced perceptions among his supporters that he was under siege from various fronts.

Legacy of Divine Intervention

Trump's presidency has left an indelible mark on American politics, characterized by deep polarization and fervent support from his base. His belief in divine intervention shaped not only his policies but also how he framed challenges during his administration. The attempts on his life further complicated his narrative of being a leader fighting against overwhelming odds and persecution. Trump's legacy includes significant tax reforms, a focus on deregulation, and an enduring impact on conservative ideology that continues to resonate in American politics today.

Impact on History

The stories of George Washington and Eric Liddell demonstrate how divine intervention has influenced individual lives and broader historical events. Washington's leadership during the Revolutionary War laid the foundation for the United States as a nation rooted in liberty and faith. Similarly, Liddell's commitment to his beliefs, both on and off the track, left an enduring legacy of integrity and service. These moments of perceived divine guidance have had ripple effects, shaping societal values and inspiring generations.

Lessons Learned

The lives of George Washington and Eric Liddell offer profound insights into the interplay of faith, resilience, and purpose, each carrying lessons that resonate deeply with modern readers. Their journeys underscore the enduring power of belief, principles, and service, illuminating how an unwavering reliance on divine providence can shape individual lives and the course of history.

Washington's unshakable faith in divine providence acted as his anchor during some of the most trying times in American history. In the crucible of war, facing what seemed like insurmountable odds, he demonstrated a profound resilience rooted in his spiritual conviction. This was not merely a passive acceptance of fate but an active reliance on the belief that a higher power guided his steps and the destiny of the fledgling nation he led. For instance, Washington's survival during the Battle of Monongahela, despite the hail of bullets that pierced his coat and killed those around him, stood as a personal testament to the protective hand of Providence. Similarly, his leadership at Valley Forge—a period marked by despair, starvation, and disease—showcased his ability to inspire hope and determination among his men, a reflection of his faith-infused leadership. These examples teach modern readers that resilience is not the absence of struggle but the courage to move forward with trust in a greater purpose.

Eric Liddell's story, meanwhile, shines as a beacon of unwavering integrity and the courage to uphold one's principles in the face of immense societal and personal pressure. His refusal to compromise his beliefs during the 1924 Paris Olympics, even at the potential cost of his athletic career, vividly demonstrates the importance of prioritizing faith and values over worldly achievements. Liddell's decision to honor the Sabbath by not running in the 100-meter race, his strongest event, affirmed his convictions and redefined success as adherence to higher principles rather than mere victory. His eventual triumph in the 400-meter race, where he broke records and stunned the world, is a lesson in the rewards of faithfulness—not necessarily in material terms but in the vindication of living a life of integrity.

Both men also exemplified a deep commitment to service, an enduring hallmark of lives guided by faith. Washington's willingness to lead the Continental Army, often at great personal cost, and later to preside over the formation of a nascent democracy, was driven by a profound sense of duty to his fellow citizens and a vision of a better future. Similarly, Liddell's missionary work in China, where he dedicated himself to the education and spiritual nourishment of others despite the dangers posed by political unrest and war, reflected a life of selfless service. Even in the internment camp where he spent his final days, Liddell continued to uplift and serve those around him, offering spiritual guidance and organizing activities to bring hope to his fellow internees. Their lives teach us that true fulfillment is often found not in personal accolades but in the impact we have on others and the legacy of service we leave behind.

Underlying their actions was a consistent recognition of divine providence, a thread that bound their lives and decisions. Both Washington and Liddell attributed their successes, and even their survival, to the intervention and guidance of a higher power. Washington's writings frequently invoked gratitude for the role of Providence in the founding of America. At the same time, Liddell's unshaken faith in God's plan remained evident despite terminal illness. This humility and acknowledgment of a greater force at work serve as a powerful reminder to modern readers of the importance of gratitude and the recognition of blessings, even amidst adversity. Their stories urge us to look beyond ourselves, see the divine threads weaving through our lives' embroidery, and approach both triumph and trial with a heart attuned to the presence of grace.

Through their unwavering faith, steadfast principles, commitment to service, and humble recognition of Providence, George Washington and

Eric Liddell offer timeless lessons. These are not merely historical anecdotes but living inspirations, urging us to confront our challenges with courage, live with integrity, serve selflessly, and remain grateful for the unseen hand that guides us through life's journey.

Connecting Past to Present

The experiences of Washington and Liddell resonate with contemporary stories of faith and divine intervention. Just as Washington's troops found hope during the Revolutionary War and Liddell's faith sustained him in a prison camp, individuals today continue to draw strength from their beliefs in the face of adversity. These stories remind us that divine intervention is not confined to the past; it continues to inspire and guide those who seek to recognize it.

We understand how faith can shape lives and societies by reflecting on historical examples of divine intervention. These narratives encourage us to look for the extraordinary in our own journeys and to trust in the unseen hand that guides us through life's challenges.

In conclusion, the stories of George Washington and Eric Liddell illuminate the profound impact of divine intervention on both individual lives and the course of history. Their unwavering faith, resilience, and commitment to their principles are powerful reminders that divine guidance can manifest in grand historical moments and personal acts of courage. As we reflect on these examples, may we find inspiration to recognize and cherish the signs of divine presence in our own lives?

Chapter 10
Embracing a Life of Faith

Faith, at its core, is a compass that guides individuals through the complexities of life. Embracing a life of faith means committing to a purpose-driven existence marked by intentionality, trust in the divine, and a willingness to engage with the world through a spiritual lens. This chapter explores how individuals can meaningfully integrate faith into their lives, offering practical steps, historical examples, and reflections to inspire purposeful living.

Living with Purpose

Understanding Purpose in Faith

Living with purpose is central to a faith-driven life. Faith illuminates the understanding that each individual has a unique calling, contributing to the greater good in alignment with divine design. This sense of purpose is deeply rooted in spiritual traditions, where believers are encouraged to use their gifts and talents to serve and glorify God.

Biblical Foundations Scriptural teachings are replete with exhortations about purpose. Ephesians 2:10 affirms, "For we are God's handiwork, created in Christ Jesus to do good works, which God prepared in advance for us to do." This verse encapsulates the notion that every individual's life is divinely orchestrated with intentionality. Similarly, Jeremiah 29:11 provides reassurance: "For I know the plans I have for you," declares the Lord, "plans to prosper you and not to harm you, plans to give you hope and a future."

Historical Examples Historical figures who lived with purpose exemplify the transformative power of faith:

- **Florence Nightingale**: Motivated by her Christian beliefs, Nightingale revolutionized nursing, turning it into a respected profession. Her faith-driven resolve helped her endure the hardships of the Crimean War and inspired reforms in healthcare worldwide.

- **Charles Dickens**: The acclaimed author channeled his literary talents into advocating for social justice. Dickens' faith influenced his works, which often highlighted themes of redemption, empathy, and the plight of the marginalized.

Practical Steps to Discovering Purpose

Discovering one's purpose involves intentional exploration and active participation in faith-based practices:

1. **Self-Reflection**: Spend dedicated time in prayer, meditation, or journaling to discern personal passions and spiritual gifts.

   o *Example*: Practicing daily gratitude prayers can help uncover the ways in which one's life is already aligned with divine purpose.

2. **Community Engagement**: Join local charities, faith-based groups, or volunteer organizations to identify areas of service where personal skills and passions align with community needs.

3. **Seek Mentorship**: Find a mentor—a pastor, spiritual leader, or elder—who can provide guidance and encouragement in discerning and pursuing one's purpose.

Practical Steps Forward

Daily Practices to Invite Divine Intervention

Living a life of faith requires cultivating habits that foster a deeper connection with the divine. Establishing daily practices helps maintain this connection, opening pathways for divine intervention. These practices are not merely routines but intentional acts of devotion that align one's spirit with God's presence and guidance.

Prayer stands as the cornerstone of a faith-driven life. Through prayer, individuals communicate with God, seeking clarity, peace, and guidance for the challenges they face. This sacred dialogue is a time of vulnerability and openness, where believers lay bare their hearts and invite divine wisdom. Ancient traditions, such as Lectio Divina, offer a structured yet profoundly spiritual approach to prayer. This practice intertwines scriptural reading, meditation, and prayer, allowing individuals to immerse themselves in God's word and discern His will. For example, setting aside ten minutes each morning to meditate on a scripture passage and pray for guidance can transform one's outlook and instill a sense of purpose for the day ahead. This deliberate time of reflection fosters a deeper awareness of God's presence in life's mundane and extraordinary moments.

Engaging regularly with scripture is another essential practice for inviting divine intervention. Holy texts serve as a source of spiritual nourishment, providing wisdom and encouragement for navigating life's complexities. For instance, Proverbs 3:5-6 reminds believers to "Trust in the Lord with all your heart and lean not on your own understanding; in all your ways submit to him, and he will make your paths straight." This passage underscores the importance of surrendering one's plans and trusting in God's sovereign direction. By incorporating a Bible reading plan into one's daily routine, individuals can explore themes and lessons that resonate with their current circumstances, drawing strength and insight from the timeless truths of scripture. This disciplined engagement deepens one's understanding of faith and reinforces the belief that God's word is a guiding light in times of uncertainty.

Faith is not merely a private affair; it manifests powerfully through action. Acts of service embody the biblical principle of loving one's neighbor and provide tangible expressions of God's love in the world. Engaging in community service, whether through volunteering at a homeless shelter, mentoring youth, or participating in environmental conservation efforts, creates opportunities to reflect God's compassion and care.

These acts of kindness, though seemingly small, have the potential to ripple outward, inspiring others and transforming communities. Service becomes a conduit for divine intervention as individuals address immediate needs and participate in God's broader work of restoration and renewal.

Keeping a gratitude journal is another profound practice for recognizing and inviting divine blessings. By documenting moments of providence, answered prayers, and even small joys, individuals cultivate an attitude of gratitude that aligns their hearts with God's goodness. This practice shifts the focus from life's difficulties to its abundant blessings, creating a fertile ground for hope and faith to flourish. For example, taking a few minutes each evening to write down three things you are thankful for can reveal patterns of God's faithfulness that might otherwise go unnoticed. These reflections serve as tangible reminders of God's hand at work, encouraging believers to trust in His continued provision and care.

Through these daily practices—prayer, scripture reading, acts of service, and gratitude journaling—individuals can create a rhythm of life that invites divine intervention and fosters a deeper connection with the Creator. Each practice, though simple in execution, holds the potential to transform hearts and minds, drawing believers closer to God and to the life of purpose He intends for them.

Community Involvement

The Importance of Community in Faith

Faith flourishes within the context of community. Being part of a faith community fosters accountability, encouragement, and shared spiritual growth. Engaging with others strengthens one's own faith while contributing to the collective good. A faith-driven life is not meant to be lived in isolation; it is within the fellowship of others that believers find deeper meaning and reinforcement of their spiritual journey.

Participation in church services and activities forms a foundational aspect of community in faith. Regular attendance at worship gatherings provides a structured opportunity for spiritual reflection and learning and fosters connections with others who share similar beliefs. Within the walls of a church, relationships are cultivated, and a sense of belonging is nurtured. Beyond the Sunday service, many churches offer small group settings such as Bible studies or prayer circles. These intimate gatherings provide space for deeper discussion, shared vulnerability, and mutual encouragement. For instance, joining a midweek Bible study enhances one's understanding of scripture and strengthens bonds with fellow participants, creating a supportive network that extends beyond the study itself.

Volunteerism represents another vital avenue through which faith communities engage with the world. Outreach programs spearheaded by these communities often aim to address pressing societal needs, such as alleviating hunger, providing education, or responding to natural disasters. By participating in such initiatives, believers can live out their faith in tangible and impactful ways. These acts of service are not merely altruistic but are deeply rooted in the principle of loving one's neighbor as oneself. Whether it is organizing a food drive, tutoring underprivileged children, or assisting in disaster relief, these efforts reflect the heart of the Gospel—serving others with humility and compassion. For many, these acts of service become transformative experiences, deepening their understanding of God's love and their role in sharing it with the world.

Building and maintaining support networks within a faith community are indispensable for navigating life's challenges. Developing meaningful relationships with fellow believers creates a safety net of emotional and spiritual support. In times of hardship, this network becomes a lifeline, offering prayer, encouragement, and practical assistance. For example, consider a woman battling illness who finds solace and strength through her church's prayer group. The group gathers regularly to uplift her in prayer, providing spiritual intercession and emotional reassurance that she is not alone in her struggle. These connections embody the communal nature of faith, illustrating how believers are called to bear one another's burdens and share in each other's joys.

The importance of community in faith cannot be overstated. Within these shared experiences of worship, service, and support, individuals encounter God's presence in profound ways. By actively engaging in a faith community, believers strengthen their own spiritual journeys and contribute to the collective growth and resilience of the body of Christ. In doing so, they participate in a divine tapestry of relationships and actions that reflect God's love and purpose for humanity.

Final Reflections and Encouragement

Faith is not a destination but a continuous journey. Embracing a life of faith requires patience, resilience, and trust in the divine plan. As individuals navigate their paths, certain principles serve as anchors:

1. Embrace Uncertainty Faith often involves stepping into the unknown. Trusting God's plan, even when it defies logic or clarity, is a hallmark of spiritual growth. Hebrews 11:1 reminds believers, "Now faith is confidence in what we hope for and assurance about what we do not see."

2. Celebrate Progress Spiritual growth is incremental. Celebrate small victories, such as moments of clarity in prayer, acts of kindness, or newfound understanding of scripture, as affirmations of God's work in your life.

3. Stay Connected Remaining engaged with faith communities provides strength and accountability. Relationships with fellow believers serve as reminders that no one journeys alone.

Conclusion

Living a life of faith demands intentionality and commitment. By understanding one's purpose, engaging in daily spiritual practices, participating in community service, and remaining open to divine guidance, individuals invite transformative experiences into their lives.

Faith is a dynamic and evolving journey with opportunities for growth, joy, and fulfillment. As readers embark on or continue their spiritual journeys, they are encouraged to seek God's presence in all things, recognizing that a life of faith is a life of profound purpose and divine connection.

"The Fastest and Easiest Way to Communicate with God is Through Prayer!"